L. M. Montgomery's

Anne of Green Gables

ADAPTED BY
M.C. HELLDORFER

ILLUSTRATED BY ELLEN BEIER

A DOUBLEDAY BOOK FOR YOUNG READERS

For Gene Namovicz, a true classic
M.C.H.

For Laurie, my kindred spirit, with love
E.B.

A Doubleday Book for Young Readers
Published by
Random House Children's Books
a division of
Random House, Inc.
1540 Broadway
New York, New York 10036

Library of Congress Cataloging-in-Publication Data
Helldorfer, Mary Claire.
Anne of Green Gables / M. C. Helldorfer ; based on the novel by L. M. Montgomery ; illustrated by Ellen Beier.
p. cm.
Summary: A simplified retelling of how Anne, an eleven-year-old orphan, comes to live on a Prince Edward Island farm and proceeds to make an indelible impression on everyone around her.
ISBN 0-385-32715-3 (trade) 0-385-90001-5 (lib. bdg.)
[1. Orphans Fiction. 2. Friendship Fiction. 3. Country life—Prince Edward Island Fiction. 4. Prince Edward Island Fiction.]
I. Montgomery, L. M. (Lucy Maud), 1874–1942. Anne of Green Gables. II. Beier, Ellen, ill. III. Title.
PZ7.H37418An 2000
[E]—dc21
99-21406
CIP

The artist wishes to thank Alissa.
The text of this book is set in 15-point Cochin.
Manufactured in the United States of America
February 2001
10 9 8 7 6 5 4 3 2 1

Some people said Matthew Cuthbert and his sister, Marilla, had lost their minds when they decided to adopt an orphan boy. But both were growing old and thought a strong boy could help with the farmwork at Green Gables.

Early in June, Matthew drove their horse and buggy to the train station to pick up the orphan. When he arrived, there was only one passenger on the platform, a skinny little girl with bright red braids.

Matthew hurried past her, for girls, big or small, terrified him. He asked the stationmaster when the train was coming in.

"It's been here and gone," the man replied. "A lady got off and left you that girl over there."

"Girl?" Matthew gasped. "It's a boy I've come for."

The last thing Matthew wanted was to question the little girl who was watching his every move with big green eyes. He didn't have to. All in one breath she said: "I suppose you are Mr. Matthew Cuthbert of Green Gables. It seems so wonderful that I'm going to live with you and belong to you. I've never belonged to anybody."

Matthew didn't know how to tell the child that she wasn't going to belong to him, either. *I'll let Marilla do it,* he thought, and helped the girl into his buggy.

The child chattered all the way to Green Gables. "This island is the bloomiest place!" she exclaimed. She reached up to the apple trees that arched above the road and made a roof of snowy blossoms. "I'm so glad I'm going to live here."

Matthew said nothing.

They drove by a pond that shimmered with the colors of the evening sky. The child sighed with pleasure. "I feel pretty nearly perfectly happy," she said.

Matthew stayed quiet.

"Of course, I can't feel *exactly* perfectly happy," she rattled on, "because, as you can see, I have red hair."

Matthew worried how the child would feel when she learned she was a mistake.

"Matthew Cuthbert!" Marilla exclaimed when they came in the door. "Who's that? Where is the boy?"

"There was no boy—only her," he replied, feeling miserable for the child.

"But we asked for a boy," his sister insisted. "We have no use for a girl."

All at once, the girl understood. "You don't want me! I should have known. No one ever did!" she said, then cried stormily. Suddenly she raised her head. "If I were beautiful, and didn't have red hair, *then* would you keep me?"

"We would keep you if you were a boy," Marilla replied. "Now stop your tears and tell us your name."

"Anne Shirley."

That night, Anne was too upset to eat her supper. At bedtime, she pulled the covers over her head and sobbed.

Down in the kitchen, Marilla and Matthew talked about what to do.

"She has to go back," Marilla said. "What good would she be to us?"

"Well now, we might be some good to her," Matthew pointed out.

Marilla was amazed. Matthew, of all people, wanted to keep a little girl? Well, Marilla didn't. The next day she and Anne set out in the buggy to see Mrs. Spencer, the lady who had brought Anne from the orphanage.

"Oh dear, oh dear, what a terrible mistake," Mrs. Spencer said to Marilla. "But, luckily, Mrs. Blewett has just been asking for an orphan girl."

"Mrs. Blewett?" Marilla had heard frightening stories about her temper.

When Mrs. Blewett arrived, she looked Anne up and down with sharp eyes. "Make no mistake about it, you'll work hard for your keep," she said.

Anne sat still as a mouse caught in a trap. Marilla saw how pale the child had become.

"Well," Marilla said, "Matthew and I haven't decided for sure about Anne. We'll think things over again and let you know tomorrow."

That evening and all the next morning, Anne held her breath, until Marilla told her —

They wanted her! They'd keep her!

Every day Anne did her chores, then explored Green
Gables. She made friends with the laughing brook and leafy
trees, the windblown buttercups and wild roses. But she
wanted people friends, too. She dreamed of having her own
best friend.

The day Marilla took her to meet their neighbors, Anne trembled. The Barrys had a daughter named Diana. "What if she doesn't like me?" Anne asked Marilla.

Anne thought Diana was beautiful. Her hair was raven black and she wore dresses with puffy sleeves, the kind Anne longed for but Marilla said cost too much. Best of all, Diana liked to pretend—as long as someone else started the imagining. And Anne was very good at that.

They became best friends and made a playhouse in a corner of land encircled by birch trees. Anne named it Idlewild. Their seats were huge stones covered with moss. Boards placed between trees made shelves. On these, they kept broken dishes and glass from a shattered lamp. Anne called it fairy glass and said the fairies had left it behind the night they had a ball.

Summer flew by, and it was almost time for the Avonlea church picnic. Anne could think and talk of nothing else.

Two days before the picnic, Marilla came downstairs looking very serious. "Anne," she said, "I can't find my amethyst pin."

"I saw it on your bureau this afternoon," Anne replied. She loved to look at the sparkling purple stone, which was Marilla's finest treasure.

"Did you touch it?"

"Y-e-e-s," Anne admitted. "I tried it on. But I put it right back."

"I have looked everywhere on the bureau and in the room as well. It's gone," Marilla told her.

"I put it back," Anne insisted. "I did, Marilla! I did!"

"It isn't there, Anne. You must have lost it. Go to your room until you are ready to confess the truth."

The morning of the picnic, Anne finally confessed. "I took the pin to our playhouse," she told Marilla. "Your amethyst is so much better for imagining than our flower necklaces. When I was coming home by the bridge, I held it up to see how prettily it glittered. Then I dropped it, deep down in the pond."

Marilla was surprised and angered by Anne's carelessness.

"Now may I go to the picnic?" Anne asked cheerfully.

"Picnic, indeed! You'll go to no picnic today. You're punished."

Anne flung herself on the bed and cried. At noontime, she would not eat.

Marilla, who had scrubbed the floors and raked the yard twice as hard that day, decided to do some quiet sewing. From her bedroom trunk she fetched her torn shawl. When she lifted it up, she saw that something had caught on the black lace—a sparkling purple stone. Marilla remembered that she had laid the shawl on her bureau, where Anne had said she'd left the pin.

Marilla carried the amethyst into Anne's room. "Look what I have found!" she said. "Now, Anne, tell me, what was that pond story all about?"

"Why, it was a confession," Anne said. "You told me I couldn't leave my room until I confessed. I wanted so much to go to the picnic!"

Marilla laughed and shook her head. "You do beat all. I was wrong to doubt you, Anne, for you have never lied to me before. Of course, it was wrong of you to confess to something you hadn't done," she added. "If you forgive me, I'll forgive you. Now get yourself ready for the picnic."

Anne flew up like a rocket.

Later that evening, Marilla told Matthew what had happened. "One thing's for certain," she said, "no house that Anne's in will ever be dull."

And no school, either, as Avonlea's teacher soon found out.

According to the girls at Avonlea school, Gilbert Blythe was the handsomest thing. He was also a terrible tease and could make all the girls squeal. Except Anne. When she wasn't doing lessons, she was looking out the window, lost in wonderful daydreams.

Gilbert wasn't used to girls ignoring him. One day he pulled Anne's long red braid. "Carrots! Carrots!" he whispered.

Anne's eyes flashed. More than anything she hated her carrot-colored hair. She sprang to her feet. "You mean, awful boy!" she shouted, and smacked him over the head with her writing slate.

"Oh!" exclaimed the others in the class.

The teacher stalked down the aisle toward Anne.

Gilbert spoke up quickly. "It was my fault, Mr. Phillips. I teased her."

But the teacher acted as if he didn't hear. "I am sorry to see such a display of temper," he told Anne. "Go to the front of the room."

On the chalkboard above her head, Mr. Phillips wrote,

Anne must learn to control her temper.

She had to stand there the whole afternoon, letting everyone see her shame.

After school, Gilbert told her he was sorry. Anne walked past him without a word. "I shall never forgive Gilbert Blythe," she said to Diana.

And for the moment, that was true.

Anne often prayed to God that he would change the color of her hair. Then, one day, she took the matter into her own hands.

Marilla had come home from a church meeting and found Matthew hungry for supper, which Anne was to have made. The house was dark and cold. Marilla hurried upstairs.

"Mercy!" she exclaimed when she discovered Anne in her room, hidden under the bedcovers. "Are you ill?"

From beneath the pillow came a muffled voice. "No. But please, Marilla, go away and don't look at me."

"Anne, whatever is the matter with you?"

The child slowly lifted her head. "Look at my hair."

"Why, it's green!" Marilla said.

"I bought some dye from a peddler," Anne explained. "He promised it would turn my hair raven black."

They washed Anne's hair every day that week, and every day it came out green. The peddler who'd sold the dye might have been wrong about the color, but he was right about another thing—it wouldn't wash out. Anne didn't go to school, for she couldn't bear to have anyone see her.

Finally Marilla got out the scissors. Anne went back to class with her hair cut as close as a lamb's.

In time, Anne's hair grew back. The skinny girl from the orphanage grew taller and wiser and prettier. Which didn't mean she stayed out of trouble—not Anne! There was the day she baked a cake for the minister and his wife and accidentally added drops of bitter medicine instead of vanilla. And another day when someone dared Anne to walk the roof; she tumbled to the ground and broke her ankle. And another when Anne sank a boat in the middle of the pond and had to be rescued by Gilbert Blythe.

But there were also times like the Christmas morning when Anne opened a special gift from Matthew. He and Marilla watched with surprise when Anne said nothing at all.

"Why—Anne—don't you like it?" Matthew asked.

"*Like* it!" she exclaimed, scooping up the dress. "Oh, I can never thank you enough. Look at those puffed sleeves. It seems to me that this must be a happy dream!"

But Matthew and Marilla's love for Anne was not a dream; it was real—a gift shared by them and the little girl who had found a home at Green Gables.